D1499901

Rebound by 1985-86 PTO

The Checker Players

by Alan Venable

illustrated by Byron Barton

J.B. Lippincott Company / Philadelphia and New York

U.S. Library of Congress Cataloging in Publication Data

Venable, Alan, birth date
The checker players.

SUMMARY: Although they have different ways of going about things, the carpenter and the tinker work out a way
of doing things together.

[1. Friendship—Fiction] I. Barton, Byron, illus. II. Title.   PZ7.V5488Ch   [E]   73-2883   ISBN-0-397-31479-5

To my father

Emerson Venable

The carpenter was the most orderly man you could imagine. His hammer was always hanging from its loop on his neatly pressed overalls. He had a pocket shaped especially for his screwdriver and another for screws right next to it. Altogether he had seventeen pockets and a tool for each one. He could make anything.

"Just show me the plans and leave it to me," he would say. "As long as I know all the details before we start, everything will come out fine."

Across the river from the carpenter lived a tinker. Jack of all trades, he called himself: mender, patcher, scissors grinder, junk collector, doodadder, potlucker, fudgeabout, and many things besides. He could do anything somehow or another, and nothing perfectly.

His trousers were wrinkled and spattered, his hat so big it sank down over his ears, and moths flew in and out of the holes. The tinker carried a gunnysack over his shoulder, full of whatever you needed.

The tinker and the carpenter had built their own houses, and they were as different as could be. The carpenter's looked like a birdhouse. It was neatly put together out of wood, with not a stray splinter.

The tinker's, on the other hand, looked more like the home of a pack rat. The walls were stacks of cartons, crates, bricks, bales, broken bookshelves, and splintery boards. The roof was tattered carpets, old school notebooks, newspapers, ripped slickers, flattened tins, and broken umbrellas. The whole thing was propped up with posts and poles and held together with baling wire, brown glue, rusty nails, Scotch tape, string, bubble gum, and a dozen other catchy, sticky things.

One Saturday the tinker called across the river.
"I say," he shouted to the carpenter, "how about a game of checkers?"

"My favorite game!" the carpenter called back. "Come right over!"

The tinker jumped into the river, clothes and all, and swam across. He clambered up the bank with water pouring from his hatbrim.

The carpenter brought out his checker set and a wooden table with matching chairs.

"I made everything myself," he said proudly, "even the checkers with the little pictures of kings carved on the tops."

"I'm very impressed," said the tinker.

They sat down to play. The carpenter was cautious. He stared at the board for ages before each move. The impatient tinker fidgeted in his seat, whistled, and tapped his fingers. Finally the carpenter won.

"I haven't had so much fun in years," the carpenter said happily. "You certainly play quickly."

"Thank you," replied the tinker. "What patience you have. Shall we play at my house next Saturday?"

"That would be fine," said the carpenter, "but I don't know how to swim."

"That's all right," said the tinker. "Give me a piece of rope. We'll tie one end here, and I'll swim across the river with the other and tie it to a tree. Come Saturday, you can pull yourself across on the rope."

"Great idea!" cried the carpenter. "How easily you think of things."
So the tinker swam home with the rope.

The carpenter was particular about not getting his clothes wet, so he made a special wooden box to carry them in. First he drew a sketch of the box, then a blueprint, with numbered instructions and a list of all the tools he would need. "I like things to come out exactly right," he said.

The following Saturday he crossed the river gripping the rope and holding his new clothes-box over his head.

He climbed out on the other side and dressed himself as the tinker came to greet him. The carpenter rubbed his hands together. "Where are the checkers?" he asked.

"My goodness!" cried the tinker. "I thought you were bringing yours. I haven't any."

"Ah," said the carpenter. "I couldn't bring my checkers *and* my clothes across the river at the same time."

"Why didn't you put the checkers inside the clothes-box?" asked the tinker.

"You don't understand," the carpenter replied. "The box wasn't *made* to hold the checker set."

"Did you try to fit it in?" the tinker persisted.

"No!" snapped the carpenter.

His anger made them both pause.

"No matter," the tinker said finally. "Just wait here."

He ran into his tumbledown house and rummaged about inside. A few minutes later he came out with an armload of stuff.

"Let's see," he said, dumping it in a pile. He picked out a hunk of cardboard and set it across a breadbox. He grabbed a checkered tablecloth and spread it over the cardboard.

"Presto!" he said. "That's the checkerboard!"

From his pockets he pulled bottle caps, buttons, peace pins, poker chips, subway tokens, and a dusty cracker or two.

"Twelve checkers for me, twelve for you," he said. "Now let's play."

They sat on orange crates and played, and this time the tinker won.

"That makes us even, doesn't it," he said smugly, removing the carpenter's last king from the board.

"I suppose so," the carpenter replied. "Of course, your so-called checkers didn't make things easy. I couldn't tell which ones were mine."

"Tut! Tut! No excuses," said the tinker.

"And your whistling and fidgeting are definitely annoying to a deep thinker like myself," the carpenter added.

"Is that so!" cried the tinker. "Well, imagine how dull it is for me when you dally over every move."

"Dally, indeed!" the carpenter yelled. "After I wore myself out crossing the river, just to please you!"

"Who crossed over last week?" the tinker bawled.

They paced back and forth, trampling the tinker's flowers.

"All right, wise guy," he challenged finally. "Use your checkers, and I'll use mine. We'll meet halfway across the river!"

"But I can't swim!" the carpenter bellowed.

"Pooh-bah!" said the tinker. "Build a boat."

"A boat?" The carpenter stopped short. "What a good idea. How did you think of that?"

"Oh, it just . . . popped out," the tinker answered.

"Very well," declared the carpenter. "You build one, too, and we *will* meet halfway!"

Neither the tinker nor the carpenter had ever built a boat before. Each set about it in his own way.

The carpenter decided on a dinghy with a cotton sail. It would be precisely six and a half feet long, and everything but the sail would be of wood. He got out his drawing board and made plans all the first day.

He knew every single thing about his boat before he so much as sharpened his saw. Then he began to build.

The tinker rummaged through his trash. He found an old piece of linoleum and said, "Say, what a great floor for my boat."

He took the root beer billboard off his roof. He discovered a broken shovel that would do for a paddle. When he came across a discarded porch awning he realized that the boat needed a roof and that this would do just fine. He collected everything that looked useful and began sticking it all together.

They worked furiously all week. A mountain of wood shavings grew up by the carpenter's bench as he planed and chiseled away, carefully following his plan.

Across the river the tinker puttered about, stacking things together, pounding carpet tacks with the heel of his shoe, gluing this to that with goopy brown paste, and stuffing the cracks with chewing gum and modeling clay.

As they worked, neither could resist running down to the riverbank to see how the other was doing and to brag.

"The best darn boat you ever saw!" the carpenter raved loudly. "Everything exactly the way I planned it, right down to the last peg!"

"Mine's got a roof!" the tinker hooted. "You can sit in the hot sun, but my boat has a roof!"

By Saturday they were ready.
The tinker pushed his contraption down to the water and dumped it in.

Immediately the boat groaned and rolled over. It floated, all right, but bottom up, with the roof under water.

"Some boat!" the carpenter guffawed from the other side. "Haw, haw, haw, haw, haw."

"It floats, doesn't it?" the tinker shouted hotly, taking his checkers and shovel in hand and stepping gingerly onto his raft.

"Now it's your turn, smarty!" he cried.

The carpenter slid his dinghy into the water; it floated as nicely as a cork. Carefully he stepped in and raised the sail.

The little craft leaned with the wind and glided smoothly out into the mainstream.

"Couldn't be more perfect!" the carpenter cried gaily, waving at the tinker.

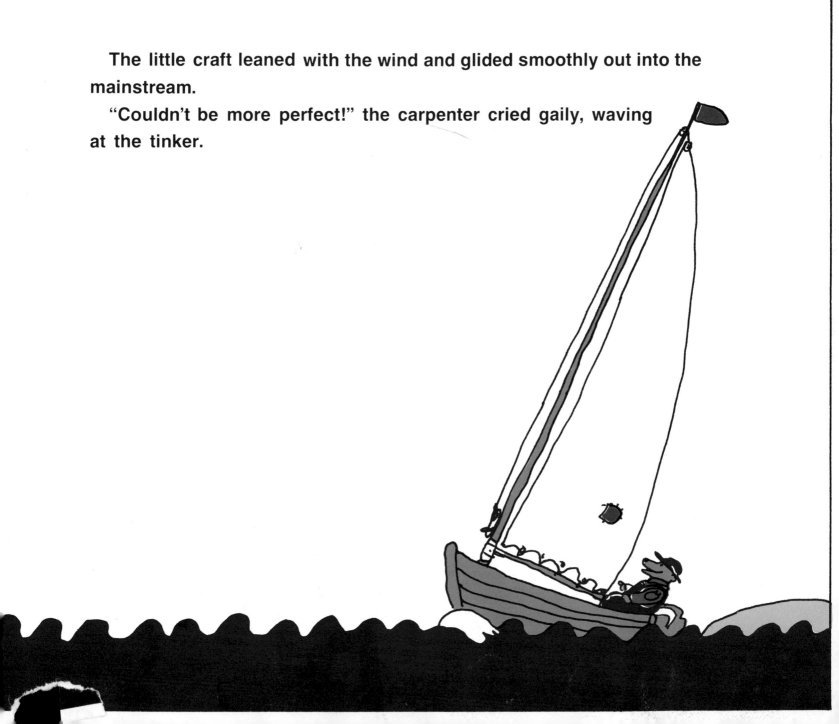

Suddenly, ooooops!

An odd puff of wind out of nowhere drove into the sail. Over went the little boat, spilling the astonished carpenter into the river.

"Help!" The poor carpenter floundered and thrashed, out of reach of the wallowing dinghy.

"Help! I can't swim!" he pleaded, going under momentarily.

"You can't sail, either!" the tinker laughed. "You left the wind out of your plans!"

"Help!" cried the carpenter once more. "I'm drowning!"

Indeed, he was. He gulped for air and disappeared a second time under the water.

"I'm coming, I'm coming! Hold your breath!" the tinker screamed, flinging away his shovel and diving in.

The carpenter thrashed to the surface and gulped one last breath. He was sinking for the third and final time.

"Good-bye, cruel world," he sobbed as the river dragged him down.

The tinker reached the drowning carpenter, caught him by the overalls and pulled him up. He grunted as he dragged his friend to shore. At last they stumbled out of the water.

They rested for a long time, while the sunshine dried them out.

"I never could swim," the carpenter said.

"No wonder," said the tinker, "you must weigh a ton."

"Yes," said the carpenter. "My tools, you know."

The tinker was astonished that the carpenter's heavy tools were still in their pockets.

"You didn't throw your tools away when you were sinking?" he asked.

"No," said the carpenter. "I didn't think of it."

"But you almost drowned," the tinker moaned.

"That's true," said the carpenter, blushing, "but that wasn't in the plan."

"Bless me, you're a strange one," sighed the tinker, stretching out.

Suddenly he had an idea.

"Say," he said, "do you think we could build a boat together?"

"Like yours or mine?" the carpenter asked.

"Like both, of course. You make a plan for another boat, big enough for two, with a cabin roof and all. We'll build it together and I'll take care of emergencies. Okay?"

"Good idea," said the carpenter.

So they built their boat, a beautiful one, and spent many days on the river together.

ALAN VENABLE was born in Pittsburgh and attended Harvard College. For almost two years he taught in Tanzania and now lives in Montreal with his wife, Gail. This is his first book for children.

BYRON BARTON is from Los Angeles, and now lives in New York City. His previous books are *Where's Al?*, *Elephant,* and *Applebet Story.*